THIS BOOK BELONGS TO:

_ _ _ _ _ _ _ _ _ _

For my wonderful siblings, Christopher,
Morgan, Allison, Ryan and Collin.

First published in 2022 by Flying Eye Books,
an imprint of Nobrow Ltd. 27 Westgate Street, London, E8 3RL.

Text and illustrations © Sarah Noble 2022.

Sarah Noble has asserted her right under the Copyright, Designs and Patents Act,
1988, to be identified as the Author and Illustrator of this Work.

1 3 5 7 9 10 8 6 4 2

Published in the US by Nobrow (US) Inc.
Printed in Poland on FSC® certified paper.

ISBN: 978-1-83874-051-1
www.flyingeyebooks.com

SARAH NOBLE

THE PERFECT ROCK

FLYING EYE BOOKS

Every otter worth their sea salt knows
the perfect rock is hard to find.

But Ollie, Bea, and Ula
don't have time to think about
rocks because, well . . .

. . . they have a busy schedule.

And, after a long day, nothing hits the spot more than a shellfish feast.

"Now all you need is something to open shells with so you can have feasts all on your own!"

Ollie, Bea, and Ula do love shellfish.

"It takes time to find the perfect rock," Papa says. "So, it's important to know what to look for."

"The perfect rock is tough," Mama says.
"Tough enough to break the hardest shells."

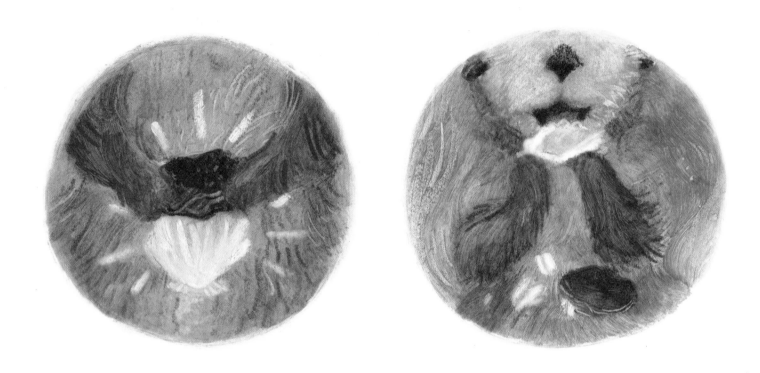

"Don't forget smooth," Papa says.
"Smooth enough to dance in your paws."

"Most importantly," they say, "Your rock must be something you hold dear, something you'll hold tight and never lose."

Together, they venture
through forests . . .

. . . and glide through skies,
in search of the perfect rock.

They search
high tide and low tide
until finally . . .

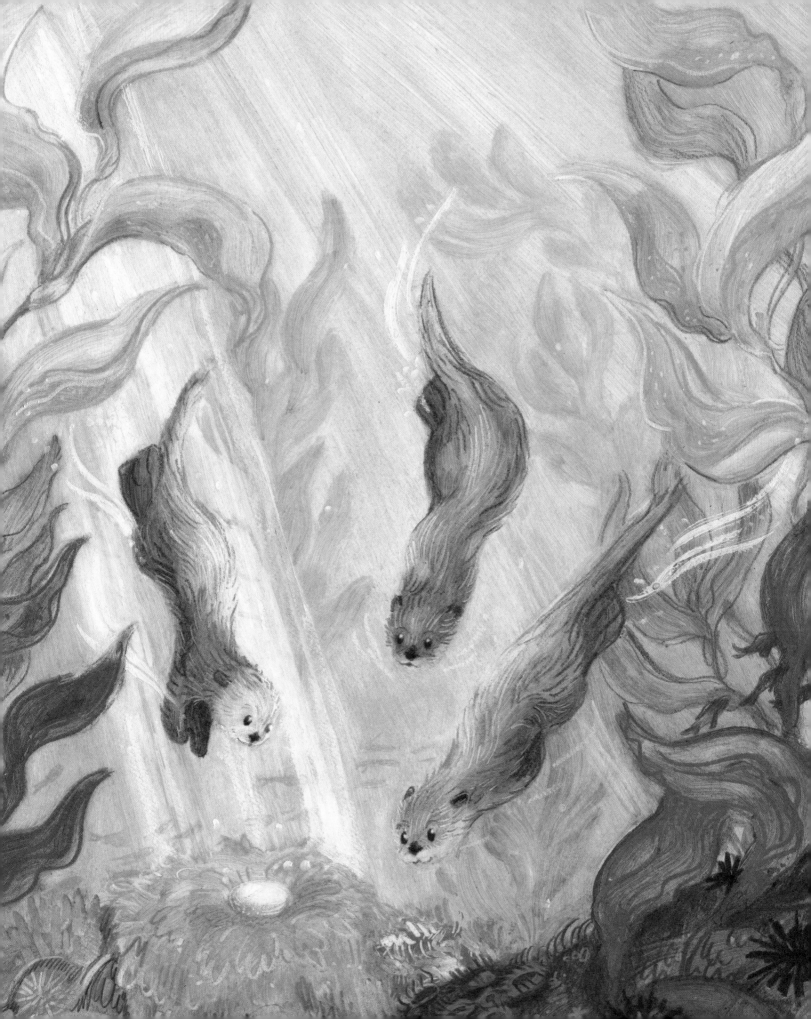

"It's tough!" Ollie says,
"Tough enough to break
the hardest shells."

"And smooth," says Bea.
"Smooth enough to dance
in my paws."

"I love it," says Ula.
They all do.

But there is only one.

"The perfect rock will fit perfectly in my pouch," says Ula.

"But I saw it first!" whines Ollie.

"But I have it now," says Bea.

"And you can't catch me!"

They spring and splash . . .

turn and twist,

fumble and . . .

. . . the perfect rock is gone.

Ollie, Bea, and Ula don't look at each other the whole
swim home. Not when they pass a slippery looking slide.

Not even when they spy a funny-looking fish.

They're too angry, and too sad.

But when the waves start moving
in a quicker, scarier rhythm,

they remember to
hold each other tight.

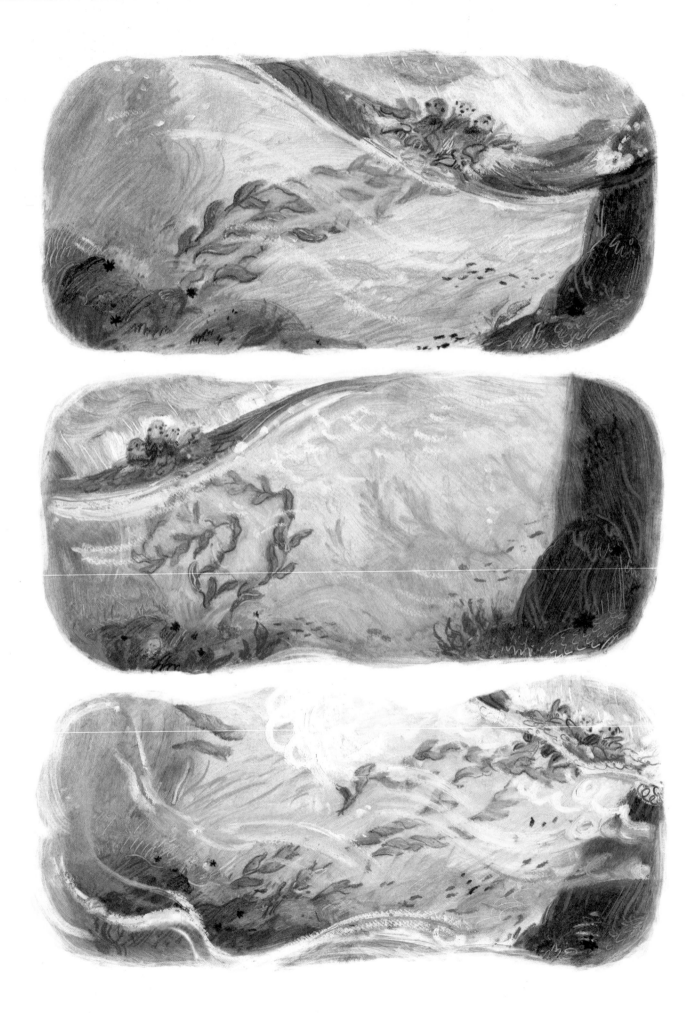

"I'm sorry," they all say,
feeling lighter already.

"Who needs that old rock
anyway?" Ollie says.

"There are lots
of rocks," Ula says.

"Maybe there's still a
perfect one for each of us."

The perfect rock is tough, tough enough to weather the storm.

It is smooth, smooth enough to ease worries big and small.

Most importantly, the perfect rock is
dear enough to hold tight and never lose.

That is what every otter worth their sea salt knows.